Enrico
Starts School

310811

For my Mum and Dad

First published in 2004 in Great Britain by Gullane Children's Books
This paperback edition published in 2005 by

Gullane Children's Books

an imprint of Pinwheel Limited
Winchester House, 259-269 Old Marylebone Road,
London NW1 5XJ

1 3 5 7 9 10 8 6 4 2

Text and illustrations © Charlotte Middleton 2004

The right of Charlotte Middleton to be identified as the author
and illustrator of this work has been asserted by her in
accordance with the Copyright, Designs and Patents Act, 1988.

A CIP record for this title is available from the British Library.

ISBN 1-86233-449-8 hardback
ISBN 1-86233-515-X paperback

Printed and bound in China

Charlotte Middleton

Enrico
Starts School

GULLANE
CHILDREN'S BOOKS

When he was four, Enrico was **brilliant** at riding his bike.

Diego,
the amazing
wind-up
mouse

He was **awfully good** at
sneaking up on Diego mouse.
And he could make a **magnificent**
pilchard in lobster-jelly sandwich.

munch

munch

Now that he was **five**, Enrico was old enough for his first day at school.

The playground looked **ever so big.**

Enrico had **no idea** how to make friends.

In class he was **too shy** to put his paw up, even though he knew some of the answers.

At breaktime, Enrico tried to join in with some cats who were playing with their remote-control mouse . . .

MOTOR MOUSE MOTOR MOUSE

cool mouse

but they were
not impressed
with Diego.

At lunchtime, Enrico sat with some other cats. He offered them a bite of his carefully-prepared pilchard in lobster-jelly sandwich . . .

but they showed **too much** interest in the sandwich . . .

empty tummy

empty lunchbox

and **not enough** interest in Enrico.

At home-time, Enrico suddenly thought of a brilliant idea for making friends . . .

The other cats challenged Enrico
to **a race** at breaktime.

Enrico started the race **slowly**.

wobbly cotton reel

But then his skates began to go **faster and faster . . .**

The roller-skates hadn't been such a good idea, after all.

Enrico decided that the next day he would just . . . be **himself**.

So, in the morning, he set off for school with a **spring in his step**.

In class he put his paw up . . .
and got the answer **right**!

At breaktime, Enrico **didn't** **really** mind playing on his own . . .

Enrico . . . being himself

but he was **very pleased** when he felt a gentle tap on his shoulder.

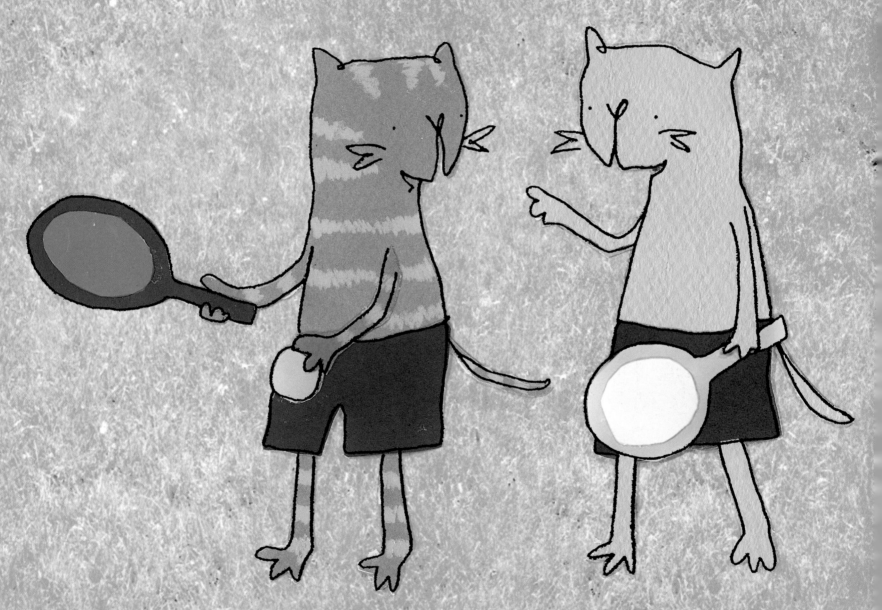

A rather shy cat said his name was Lucas and asked if he could play with Enrico.

great rally!

In no time at all, Enrico and Lucas

had become the best of friends.

best
buddies

After school, Enrico invited Lucas
to play at his house.

little
chums

Pablo was playing with a new friend.
It was **Miguel**, Lucas's little brother.

Enrico, Lucas, Pablo and Miguel spent all afternoon making an exciting course for Enrico's model train set . . .

and Enrico's pilchard in lobster-jelly sandwiches were the **most magnificent** he had ever made.